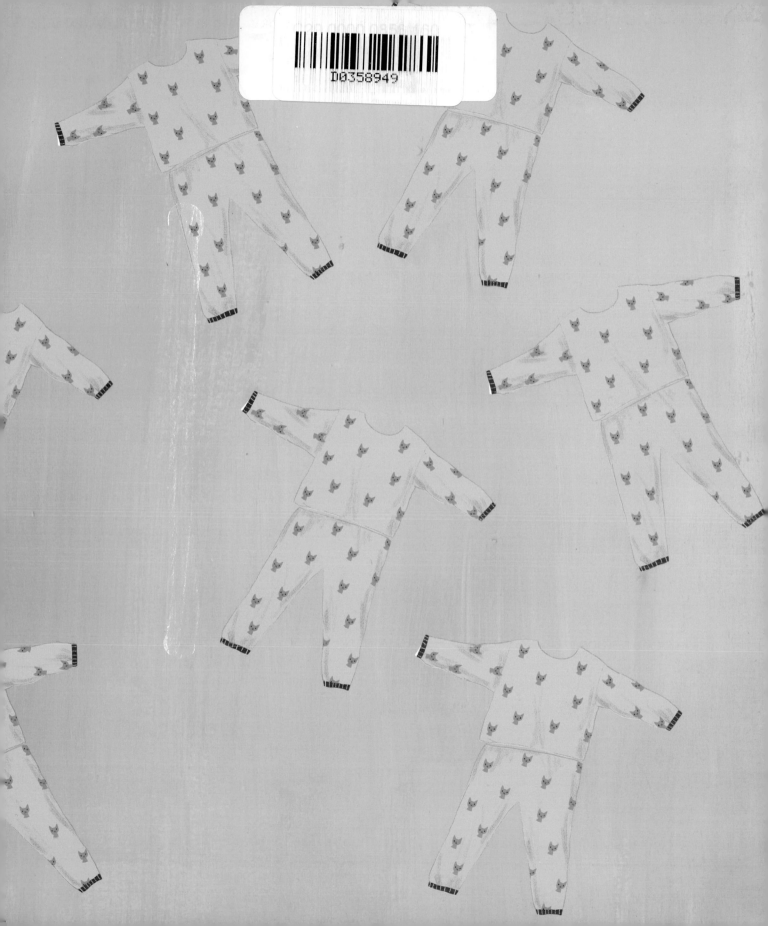

For Cathy - even though she wouldn't give me her slappy silver sandals - A. MQ
For Lianna and Nathanael, with love - R.B

With special thanks to Kathelene Iagrossi Arhin-Acquaah, Rhianna, Channara, Katouche, Aisha and Fiona for their insights

 Find Booky Girl Lulu activities and more on our website. Scan the code or visit the activities and resources page at www.alannamax.com

First published in the UK & Ireland by Alanna Max
38 Oakfield Road, London N4 4NL
Lulu's Sleepover © 2021 Alanna Max
Text copyright © 2021 Anna McQuinn
Illustrations copyright © 2021 Rosalind Beardshaw
Lulu's Sleepover is part of the Booky Girl Lulu series
developed by and published under licence from Anna McQuinn.
www.AnnaMcQuinn.com
All Rights Reserved.
www.AlannaMax.com

Printed in China
ISBN 978-1-907825-38-5 HB

123456789

Lulu's
Sleepover

by Anna McQuinn
Illustrated by Rosalind Beardshaw

Alanna Max

Tonight is Lulu's first sleepover!
Lulu has visited her cousin Hani lots of times,
but she has never stayed overnight.

Lulu wants to wear her favorite kanga dress.
Then she chooses what else to bring.

Lulu packs her leggings for jumping.
She packs her dungarees for building.

Lulu and Hani will be dancing, too. Her twirly
dress and sparkly shoes are essential for that.

Lulu packs her cat pajamas and her best books. Mary-Mary and Dinah go on top. Lulu is ready.

Hani's house is just around the corner.
Lulu and her daddy walk there.

Auntie Zari welcomes them.

Hani and Auntie Jina are making lemonade.
Lulu can't wait to taste it.

Daddy kisses everyone goodbye.
He will be back in the morning.

Hani and Lulu play in Hani's rainforest.

They build bridges and make a waterfall.
It is awesome.

Then Hani and Lulu make water pictures.
They paint the whole wall...

and each other!

Hani and Lulu play dress-up after lunch.
Now Lulu is Hani...

and Hani is Lulu!

Auntie Jina has made Hani's favourite salad for dinner.

Lulu has never liked cucumbers, but these ones are delicious!

There is just enough time for a movie before bed.

Hani's bed is magical.
Lulu takes out Mary and Dinah.
Her place is all set.

Auntie Zari has a surprise. It is a photo album of when Auntie Zari and Lulu's daddy were little.

Auntie Zari tells them
a special bedtime story
about the photos.

Good morning! It is time for Hani and Lulu to wake up.

Hani loves French toast. Auntie Jina makes some as a special treat. Lulu tries it. Mmmm! Delicious!

Ding-dong! It is Daddy already.
He has come to pick up Lulu.

Lulu loved her sleepover.
Soon it will be Hani's turn to come
to Lulu's house! Lulu can't wait!

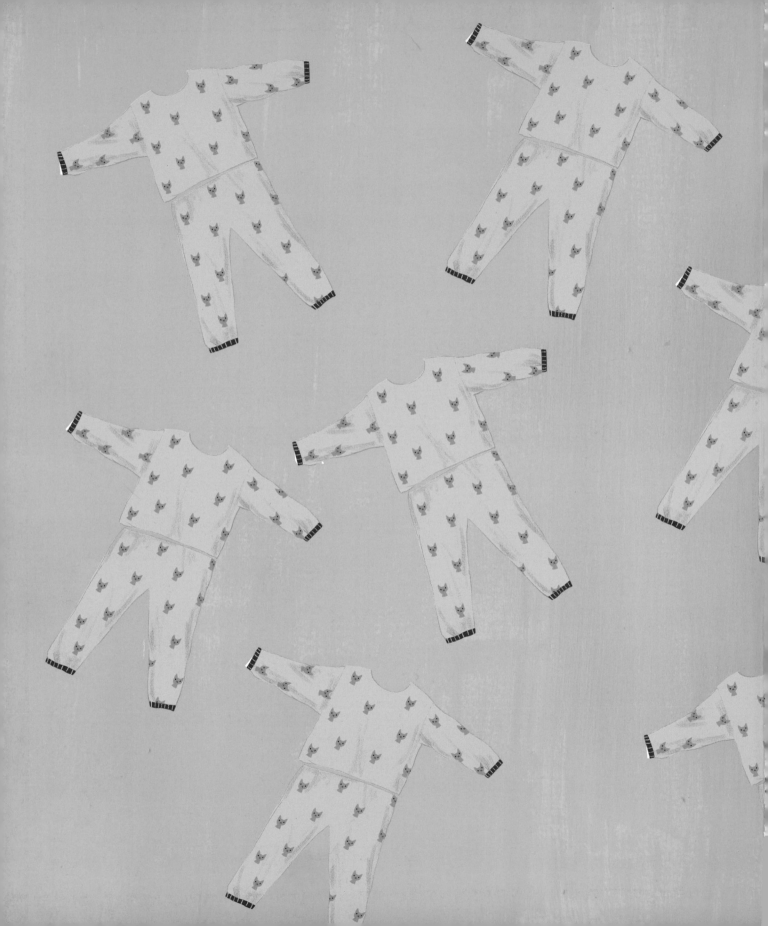